The
Dancing
Bear

michael morpurgo

The
Dancing
Bear

Illustrated by

CHRISTIAN BIRMINGHAM

HarperCollins *Children's Books*

First published in Great Britain by Collins in 1994
HarperCollins *Children's Books* is a division of HarperCollins*Publishers* Ltd,
77-85 Fulham Palace Road, Hammersmith, London W6 8JB

The HarperCollins *Children's Books* website address is
www.harpercollinschildrensbooks.co.uk

37

Text copyright © Michael Morpurgo 1994
Illustrations copyright © Christian Birmingham 1994

The author and illustrator assert the moral right to be identified as the author and
illustrator of the work.

ISBN 0 00 674511 3

Printed and bound in England by Clays Ltd, St Ives plc

For Gina and Murray, with thanks

THE DANCING BEAR

I was born in this mountain village longer ago than I like to remember. I was to have been a shepherd like my grandfather and his grandfather before him, but when I was three, an accident left me with a limp. Shepherding wasn't ever going to be possible, so I became a teacher instead.

For nearly forty years now, I have been the schoolmaster here. I live alone in a house by the school, content with my own company and my music. To play my hunting horn high in the mountains, and to hear its echo soaring with the eagles, is as close as I have been to complete happiness.

Yet I suppose you could say that I became a sort of shepherd after all: I shepherd children instead of sheep, that's all. I teach them, and I'm a kind of uncle to them even after they've left school. They think I'm a bit eccentric — I play my horn and I talk to myself more than I should. Like all children, they can be a bit cruel from time to time. They call me "Three Legs" or "Long John Silver" when they think I'm not listening, but you have to put up with that.

We are people whose lives are ruled by sheep, by the seasons, and above all by the mountains. We make cheese here, sheep's cheese. You won't find a better cheese anywhere, that's a promise. Almost all the families have a flock of sheep which they graze in the fields around the village, but when the snows clear, they take them up on to the mountain pastures for the sweet summer grass. The cows go too, and the horses and the pigs.

Snow cuts us off for at least three months of every winter, sometimes more, and then we are left to ourselves. But it's a peaceful place at any time of year. The winding road from the valley ends in the village square. Beyond us are the mountains, and beyond the mountains, the sky. We are a world of our own and we like it that way. We are used to it. The life is hard but predictable. People are born, people die. We have our blizzards and our droughts, no one ever has enough money and the roof always needs repairing.

Nothing ever really disturbed our life until some ten years ago, when a small bear came down out of the mountains. Nothing was ever to be the same again.

Roxanne was about seven years old at the time. An orphan child, she lived with her grandfather, who was a dour and unloving man. She was a solitary girl, but never lonely, I think. At school, she appeared to be a dreamer, a thinker. After school, with her grandfather busy in his fields, she would often wander off by herself, watching rabbits, maybe, or following butterflies. She was forever going missing. Then her grandfather would come shouting around the village for her. When he found her, he would shake her or even hit her. I protested more than once, but was told to mind my own business. A friendless, bitter old man, Roxanne's grandfather was interested in nothing unless there was some money in it. Roxanne was a nuisance to him. She knew it – and everyone knew it. But he was the only mother and father she had.

It was a Sunday morning in April. We were in the café before lunch. The old man was going on about Roxanne again, and how she ate him out of house and home. He'd had a bit too much to drink, I think, but then he was often that way.

"Gone off again, she has," he grumbled. "God knows what she gets up to. Nothing but trouble, that girl."

Just then we heard shouting in the village square and, glad of any diversion, we all went out to look. Roxanne was staggering towards us, clutching a bear cub in her arms, with its arms wrapped around her neck. She'd been scratched on her face and on her arms, but it didn't seem to bother her. She was laughing and breathless with joy.

"Bruno!" she said. "He's called Bruno. I was down by the stream. I was just throwing sticks and I felt something stroking my neck. I turned round and there he was. He patted my shoulder. He's my very own bear, Grandpa. He's all alone. He's hungry. I can keep him, can't I? Please?"

If we hadn't been there – and half the village was there by now – I think the old man might have grabbed the bear cub by the scruff of the neck and taken him right back where he came from.

"Look at him," he said. "He's half starved. He's going to die anyway. And besides, bears are for killing, not keeping. You know how many sheep we lose every year to bears? Dozens, I'm telling you, dozens."

Some people were beginning to agree with him. I looked at Roxanne and saw she was looking up at me. Her eyes were filled with tears.

"Maybe" — I was still thinking hard as I spoke — "if you kept him, you know, just for a while. It wouldn't cost much: some waste milk and an old shed somewhere. And just suppose" — I was talking directly to the old man now — "just suppose you made 'bear' labels for your honey jars — you could call it 'Bruno's Honey'. Everyone would hear about it. They'd come from miles around, have a little look at the bear and then buy your honey. You'd make a fortune, I'm sure of it."

I'd said the right thing. Roxanne's grandfather had his beehives all over the mountainside, and everyone knew that he couldn't sell even half the honey he collected. He nodded slowly as the sense of it dawned on him. "All right," he said. "We'll try it. Just for a while, mind."

Roxanne looked at me and beamed her thanks. She went off with Bruno, followed by an excited cavalcade of village children who took turns to carry him.

That afternoon, they made him a bed of bracken at the back of one of the old man's barns, and fed him a supper of warm ewe's milk from a bottle. They dipped his paw in honey and made him suck it. After that he helped himself. Later when I passed by the barn on my evening walk, I heard Roxanne singing him to sleep. She sang quite beautifully.

In no time at all, Bruno became one of the village children; nobody was afraid of him, as he was always gentle and biddable. He'd go splashing with them in the streams; he'd romp with them in the hay barns; he'd curl himself up in a ball and roll with them helter-skelter down the hillsides. He was more than a playmate, though. He was our mascot, the pride of the village.

To begin with, he never strayed far from Roxanne. He would follow her everywhere, almost as if he were guarding her. Then one day – and by this time, Roxanne was maybe ten or eleven – he broke out of his barn and followed her to school.

I was sitting at my desk sharpening pencils and the class was settled at its work, when Bruno's great panting face appeared at the window, tongue lolling out and drooling. Roxanne managed to shut him in the woodshed where he stayed till lunch, happily sharpening his claws on the logs.

Not much school-work was done *that* day.

After that Bruno was forever escaping from his barn and turning over the dustbins in the village. He liked dustbins.

But as the bear grew bigger and stronger, there were those in the village who began to worry – and I was one of them. He went walkabout again not long afterwards, and all the children were out looking for him. Tiny – the smallest boy in the school – came upon Bruno outside the village shop, his head in the dustbin. Tiny called, and Roxanne and the others came running. By the time they arrived, Bruno was up on his back legs and Tiny was tickling his tummy. Bruno swiped playfully at Tiny but it was enough to send him reeling backwards, hitting his head on a wall as he fell. The cut needed eight stitches. Roxanne swore it wasn't Bruno's fault, that it was just an accident. So did Tiny, so did they all.

That evening there was a village meeting in the café. Everyone who spoke up was adamant. Tiny's mother was furious: Bruno would have to go to a zoo. It was just too risky to keep him. Even Roxanne's grandfather agreed, and no one had expected *that*. We all knew how well he was doing out of his "Bruno's Honey."

"Honey's one thing," he said, "but a bear like that is worth a lot of money to a zoo. And he's my bear, remember?"

Suddenly Roxanne was on her feet.

"NO!" she cried. "You can't!" And she looked at me again, just as she had done all those years before.

This time there was no help I could offer her. I turned away.

"I'll look after him," she pleaded. "Honest I will. We could build a proper cage somewhere. And I won't let him out unless I'm with him. He won't hurt anyone ever again, I promise."

She spoke as if her life depended on it, and we listened. To this day, I don't know how she did it, but within minutes we were all discussing how the cage was to be paid for. Perhaps it was because everyone trusted Roxanne and liked her. She was in some way a child of the village, everyone's child; we had all seen how well she handled Bruno, how she'd sing to him to calm him and how he'd listen mesmerised, how he'd follow her everywhere adoringly. Or perhaps it was because no one liked the idea of the old man selling Bruno and pocketing the cash. Anyhow, Bruno stayed.

The cage was built in the village square and Bruno moved in. Roxanne looked after him as she had promised.

Every day, she laid fresh bracken in his den at the back of the cage, and gave him fresh water, fresh vegetables and fresh fish. I would help her catch trout in the stream and the vegetables were supplied from all over the village.

Then someone wrote an article about Bruno in a local newspaper and there was a piece on the radio. People flocked to the village to see the bear, and the old man's honey sold out in a few weeks. He bought more hives. After that there was never another mention of selling Bruno. He had a notice put up on the cage door, with a large collection box underneath:

Bruno
European Bear
Help Save Threatened Species
Donations in the box please.

The box filled fast. There were more newspaper articles and a programme on the television. People came in droves. Now it wasn't just honey they could buy: there was "Bruno's Jam", "Bruno's Beeswax", even "Bruno Teddy Bears" in rose-pink, lavender-blue or bear-brown. Roxanne's grandfather was raking in the money.

Roxanne took no notice of any of this. So long as Bruno was happy, she was too. She lived for the moment after school each day, when she would let him out of his cage and they would run together across the fields.

Often I saw them sitting together on a hillside. She'd be talking to him or singing to him, and when she sang now, she shamed even the skylarks to silence. Roxanne sang as I hope the angels sing.

I saw less of her these days. She was no longer a girl, but a young woman. She had long since left the village school for the big school in the valley. But somehow I had become her "bear-sitter". If she couldn't be there to feed Bruno, she would ask me to do it. It wasn't often and I felt honoured to be so trusted.

Bruno was always anxious when she was away. I would sing to him softly as she did, and in spite of my crusty old voice, it seemed to calm him a little. But he would always pace up and down when I left and refuse to settle until Roxanne returned.

It was at the Spring Council Meeting last year that the Mayor read out the letter. A film company, who called themselves "Wonderment Films", had written to us. The village, they said, was an ideal location for their film. They had heard about Bruno and would want to use him too. They would need accommodation for the film crew for a few days and they would need the people of the village as extras. They would need transport, they would need food. Just what sort of a film it was going to be wasn't explained.

Most of us were quick to agree to it. After all, there would be money in it for everyone. There was even some talk of actually "starring" in the film. Monsieur D'Arblay, the Mayor, said he'd done a bit of acting in his day.

"Of course, it was some time ago," he said, "but it's like riding a bicycle. Once learned, never forgotten. Let them come. That's what I say."

Everyone agreed. A letter was written and sent. The village hummed with anticipation.

The Mayor did his best to ensure the benefits would be shared. No one was allowed to rent out more than one room, and the hire of tractors, trailers, porters and guides was spread around the village as fairly as possible. Even so, there were already rumblings that some were going to do better out of the film that others. Everyone knew that. Roxanne's grandfather would be getting the lion's share – or rather the *bear's* share.

Roxanne, like all the young people in the village, could think of little else but the arrival of the film crew. In school the children were as high as kites and quite impossible to teach.

When the film crew arrived at last, late one afternoon, they were not at all as any of us had imagined. They stood in the village square, dusty, tousled and tired, and laden down with all sorts of high-tech equipment. But their clothes. . .! Bright and gaudy, coats all colours of the rainbow, lime-green shoes, pink trousers – and one glorious purple fedora hat. We all stared wide-eyed.

At first no one noticed the slight young man who stood stretching in the village square. He spoke – and it was a voice we all recognised.

"Where's the bear, then?" he demanded, looking at the cage. It was empty. Roxanne had taken Bruno for his walk.

"Niki," someone whispered, and then someone else, louder this time. "That's Niki. It's Niki, Niki, Niki, *Niki*." The name spread through the village like wildfire. No one said, "Niki who?" because everyone knew him at once, even me. Niki was just Niki, as Elvis was Elvis and George Michael was George Michael. The whole world knew Niki. Even in our remote valley, television and radio had beamed his face and his voice into every household. We couldn't take our eyes off him. That voice, that face, had suddenly become flesh.

"Where's the bear?" he said again, and at that moment Roxanne came into the square, with Bruno ambling along behind her. Bruno saw the film crew and reared up on his hind legs. They backed away. From a safe distance, Niki looked Bruno up and down. "Can he dance?" he said.

Roxanne was speechless. Like the rest of us, she could not believe that Niki was standing there in front of her – and actually *talking* to her.

"Dance," said Niki, again. "Can he dance? I need a dancing bear."

"Oh, he'll dance all right," said Roxanne's grandfather, rubbing his hands. "That bear can do anything you ask, can't he, Roxanne?"

Roxanne said nothing. She didn't need to. The anger in her eyes said it all.

★

Later that evening, we all discovered what sort of a film it was going to be. I was a little disappointed. I had had visions of some great and glamorous epic in period costume, with a battle or two; or perhaps a musical extravaganza where world-famous stars would caper through meadows and up mountainsides – *our* meadows and our mountainsides.

The Director, who turned out to be the one with the purple fedora hat, was quick to dispel such hopes. They were making a short video to accompany Niki's latest pop song, which was to be called, "Follow Me". This was greeted with screams of delight by the children (who were becoming wilder by the minute).

And, the Director went on, they would need actors – all the children he could find.

And they wanted rats.

"Rats!" Madame D'Arblay protested indignantly. "We do *not* have any rats here."

"You soon will," the Director laughed. "You soon will."

I rather liked him, or maybe it was just his wonderful hat.

"Auditions will be held in the morning. We'll be needing grown-ups for the Mayor and Corporation. Nine o'clock in the square."

Madame D'Arblay went off home at once, swearing that no child of hers would be playing a rat. Not for Niki, not for all the tea in China.

It didn't take a genius to work out that with a Mayor, Corporation and all those rats, the film was going to be something to do with the Pied Piper of Hamelin. As I lay in my bed that night, I dared to hope that I wasn't too old to play the Piper himself. I could play the flute a little, or maybe they'd even let me play my horn.

In the cold light of the following morning, the children lined up for auditions in the square. Every child in the village had volunteered. I was proud of that. I hoped Madame D'Arblay's boy would be chosen as a rat: I loved to see Madame D'Arblay angry. She had several chins and they all wobbled when she was cross.

Bruno sat and watched from his cage. I could see he was agitated.

Most of the children, including Roxanne, wanted to be rats. The whiskered costumes looked wonderful.

Niki and the Director (who brandished that purple fedora hat rather too flamboyantly for my liking) inspected the line of children, stopping to consider each one closely. Then, after a brief whispered discussion, the Director passed along the line again, picking out his chosen rats as he went: "You're a rat. A rat. Rat. Rat. Rat."

Young or old, they all wanted to be rats. Roxanne was not among those chosen nor, unfortunately, was Madame D'Arblay's boy, and neither was Tiny. They didn't hide their disappointment.

The lucky ones were hustled away into the café, which had been taken over by the Wardrobe Mistress. Here they were to be transformed into rats of all shapes and sizes. Soon after, they emerged, "ratted-up" and giggling. The Director hushed them with a wave of his hat saying he would have no noisy rats in Niki's film. Instantly, they were silent.

The Director turned to Roxanne and the others, who were still waiting miserably. "The rest of you will be the children," he declared.

"We already are," said Tiny.

Niki laughed, and when Niki laughed, everyone laughed.

"Can any of you sing?" asked the Director.

I was about to speak up, but Tiny did it for me.

"Roxy can," he said. "You should hear her. You can, can't you, Roxy?"

"A bit," said Roxanne. "We all can."

"Good, good," the Director went on. "Now I need someone to limp. . ."

A few heads turned towards me and smiled sheepishly. I smiled too. The Director pointed at Tiny. "Can you limp?"

"I think so," said tiny, and he walked up and down, limping first on one foot and then on the other.

"I'll teach Tiny," I said. "I do it quite well."

The smiles turned to laughter.

"Magic, magic!" said the Director, a bit flustered now. "This boy can be the little one who gets left behind."

It was indeed to be the story of the Pied Piper!

"Eva!" The Director shouted to the Wardrobe Mistress, a handsome woman with a mass of red hair – too red to be real – "Eva, this one will be the waif. You can get him kitted out. You can get them all kitted out. Now, I need a Mayor."

Of course, everyone looked at Monsieur D'Arblay.

"Hmmm," said the Director, looking him up and down. Clearly *our* Mayor wasn't exactly what he had in mind. "I suppose you'll do. A bit of make-up here, and a bit of padding there. We'll make a proper Mayor of you."

The Mayor didn't look too happy at this, but he accepted the part eagerly enough.

"Now," said the Director, "I want to see all the ladies. I'll need ladies who can scream — about half a dozen will do. And you've got to be able to pick up your skirts and run."

It turned out they could all scream and run well enough, so they were all chosen except Madam D'Arblay, and *she* was cast as the Mayor's wife so she was happy.

After that, the Corporation chose itself, for there were only a few of us willing to be dressed up in long flowing robes trimmed with fur. I was one — and so was Roxanne's grandfather. It was better than nothing. Of course, Niki was to be the Pied Piper so any hopes of stardom were dashed.

Most of the children were prettied and preened to look like dolls. But Tiny, who was usually so tidy, was transformed into a grubby beggar, complete with crutch. His mother kept trying to smarten him up, so the Wardrobe

Mistress had to be very firm with her. "I want him to be mucky," she insisted. "He has to be mucky."

Tiny was clearly delighted to be mucky, and together we practised his limping for hours. In the end, he was limping well. Not as well as me, but well enough.

Roxanne had never much bothered about what she looked like. Now she emerged from the café in a light-blue chiffon dress with a garland of eglantine roses in her hair. For a few moments everyone stopped and stared. She was a princess – a country girl turned into a princess in ten minutes! Yet she seemed so sad and preoccupied. She wandered over towards Bruno's cage.

I was about to go over to her when her grandfather came scurrying out of the café.

"Roxanne," he called, "they want the bear spruced up. You've got to brush him, comb him out."

She looked up at him with open dislike.

"I won't make him dance. I won't," she said. "You know I never make him do anything he doesn't want to. You know he hates being laughed at."

"What's a little dance here and a little dance there?" said the old man, with a shrug of his shoulders. "Puts money in the bank, doesn't it? That's what counts in this life and don't you forget it."

Roxanne opened the cage and stepped inside.

"Money doesn't grow on trees, you know," her grandfather went on. "Mind you have him looking his best."

And the next day, Bruno was indeed looking his best for rehearsals. We all were. But from the start, things went wrong. The carnival mood of the auditions and costuming had gone.

One by one, difficulties became problems and problems became arguments. Bruno was the worst problem of all. For some reason yet unknown to me, the Pied Piper had to have a dancing bear. Someone put a chain around Bruno's neck so that Niki could lead him into the village square. Bruno had never been chained in all his life. He would not move, and when they jerked on his chain, he reared up threateningly. Roxanne told them, we all did, that you couldn't treat Bruno like that; but they wouldn't listen.

Niki sang his song but Bruno sat stock still and looked the other way, scratching himself. They wanted him to dance and kept waving their arms at him to encourage him, but Bruno didn't even look interested. And this was just the beginning of the Director's troubles.

The children learned Niki's song and sang it well enough but they would not behave as he wanted them to. They would keep looking at the camera and giggling. The rats were no better, falling over each other because they couldn't see properly through the eye-holes in their costumes. Tiny's limping went to pieces. He *would* limp on different legs. And the more the Mayor and the Corporation rehearsed, the more self-conscious and stiff we all became.

The Director blamed everyone: the cameraman, the sound man, the weather – even, at one point, Niki. By late afternoon he was talking of abandoning the whole project, packing up and going home. Eva, the red-headed Wardrobe Mistress, was in tears because he shouted at her once too often.

We rehearsed for five minutes and stood around for five hours waiting. Filming, I decided, was hard on the feet, mostly boring and definitely bad on the nerves. We all went home thoroughly fed up and dreading doing it all again the next day.

After supper, I was just going out for my evening stroll when I heard someone singing. It could only be Roxanne. No one sang like she did. She often sang to Bruno in the evenings before she said goodnight to him. The sound of her singing drew me down towards the village square. Roxanne was sitting in the cage with Bruno standing beside her, and she was singing Niki's song. I looked across the square. Niki was listening outside the café, the Director behind him. The entire film crew was there too. Roxanne saw none of them. As I watched, Bruno began to sway from side to side. Then Roxanne was on her feet and dancing too.

When it was over, Niki started to clap loudly, and then everyone did. I did too — I couldn't help myself. Roxanne was caught quite unawares. She was embarrassed, even a little afraid, I thought.

"That girl's magic!" exclaimed the Director as he hurried past me. "Pure magic." He liked that word.

"Did you see? He was dancing!" said Niki. "The bear, he was dancing!" Niki grasped the Director's arm and they stopped close by me. "I have an idea," he whispered.

"So have I," said the Director. "And if your idea's the same as my idea, then it's brilliant."

"We sing it together, right? Her and me," said Niki.

"Her and you together," said the Director. "We'll hardly need to change a thing. You come to the village, just like we planned — a wandering minstrel with your bear — but you've got a girl with you, your girl. You do the song together. The bear dances. The children come out and dance, then the rats too. They've got to dance. They can't stop. The Mayor and Corporation see what's happening and ask you to rid them of their rats. You and the girl, with the bear behind you, you lead the rats out of the village and drown them. And then the beggars won't pay you. So you and the girl start singing again and the bear starts dancing and the children dance and they follow you both out of town and up into the mountains."

"Do you think she'll do it?" said Niki.

The Director laughed. "Do it? Of course she will. What girl wouldn't, eh? The chance to sing with Niki. And think of the publicity! Niki and his shepherdess fresh from the mountains and a bear that dances. I'm telling you, it's a winner, Niki, a winner. Sell millions. Go on, you go and ask her; and don't take no for an answer. I'll see to the grandfather. He's a tight-fisted old goat, but I'll make him an offer he won't refuse."

I stood and watched from the shadows as Niki walked over to the cage. Roxanne was just closing the door behind her. She turned and saw him. "You startled me," she said.

"With a voice like that," said Niki, "you shouldn't be stuck away up here."

"What do you mean?"

He reached out and took her hands in his. "I want to ask you a favour," he said, his voice silky soft. "I want you to sing with me — you know, in the video."

"Me?" said Roxanne.

"When you sing," Niki went on, "everyone listens. When you sing the bear dances. I must have a dancing bear, and he only dances for you, doesn't he? I need you to sing with me, Roxanne. I need you."

"I don't know," she said shaking her head.

"It's easy," Niki went on. "You sing it like you did just now, but with me." He lifted her chin so that she could look him in the eyes. "You could be a star, Roxanne. You could be big, the biggest. Look what it's done for me. Everyone knows me. I've got houses all over the world: Paris, California, south of France. I've got four cars. I've got a plane. I can have anything I want. I can go anywhere I please. You could be the same. You could leave all this behind."

"No," she said turning away from him. "I can't leave Bruno; I won't."

"Of course you can," he said. "Someone else could look after him. You can't live your life for a bear. There's a whole big wide world out there waiting to hear your voice. They'll love you. I'm telling you, Roxanne, they'll love you."

"Love me?" she said. "Will they really love me?"

Bruno was pacing up and down frantically in his cage behind them. He understood every word, I knew he did.

She smiled nervously at Niki. "I'm not sure," she said. "I live here. I belong here."

"No one belongs anywhere," said Niki. "And who wants a little place like this when you can have the whole world? I tell you what. You come with us when we leave, and if you like you can always come back. But I'm telling you, you won't want to. There're things out there you never even dreamed of and they'll all be yours. What do you say?"

"And I can have all I've ever dreamed of?" said Roxanne.

"All of it," said Niki.

If there was a moment I should have spoken up, it was then, but I hadn't the courage to do it.

I lay awake all that night telling myself I had to warn her – I *had* to stop her from going. I had to tell her. She mustn't leave. She couldn't leave. She'd be like a fish out of water. I made up my mind: I would not let her leave.

★

But when I arrived at dawn in the square, wearing my Corporation cloak, and still fully determined to say my piece, Roxanne was already rehearsing with Niki and, much to everyone's delight, Bruno was swaying and dancing as she sang.

It was too late. There was nothing I could do. At least, that was what I told myself.

Now rehearsals went like clockwork. By lunchtime they were already filming. The ladies screamed as they should, the rats ran in packs along the streets and didn't trip over, the children sang and danced just as children do, and the Mayor and the Corporation looked suitably scheming and smug. (Madame D'Arblay's chins wobbled wonderfully.)

Niki and Roxanne and Bruno led the procession of singing children into the hills never to return. And when Tiny came back, limping just the way I'd taught him, and told everyone that the children had gone for ever, it brought real tears to our eyes.

That last evening, there was a spontaneous party outside the café, brought on, I think, by relief that the film was finished, but also by a genuine friendship that had grown up between ourselves and the film crew. The children, some still in costume, were cavorting to raucous music with a thunderous pulsating beat, which the Sound Engineer had contrived to blast all around the village.

The Mayor, determined to show them that

there was another kind of music, went off to fetch his pipes. Someone pulled the plug on the amplifier and the Mayor struck up a country dance. It wasn't long before the film crew, under Madame D'Arblay's instructions, were dancing our way. They were very good at it, Niki in particular. But then, of course, we had to return the compliment and I found myself dancing

with Eva, the red-headed Wardrobe Mistress, who proceeded to teach me to dance their way. I think she'd taken a bit of a shine to me. I swear I moved parts of me I never even knew I had and I'm afraid I made a bit of a spectacle of myself. I told her of my passion for the Director's purple fedora and she laughed and ruffled my hair – no one had done that to me since I was a boy.

I would have enjoyed it all a great deal more, but all the time I could see Roxanne sitting in Bruno's cage. She was grooming him and talking to him. I knew then what she was telling him.

I was sitting at a table trying to get my breath back, when I saw Niki leave the party and go over towards her. They talked earnestly for some moments, through the bars of the cage. Then he brought her back into the café and danced with her. There was a new light in her eyes as she looked up at him, and she was more radiant than I had ever seen her.

The dancing, ancient and modern, alternated all evening. For all that time, Niki hardly left Roxanne's side. I ate too much and I drank far too much. As night fell, I went off for my usual walk. I was going back towards the square, when I saw Bruno pacing up and down in his cage as he always did when he was upset. I went over to him and sang a little, trying to calm him down. He stood by me, breathing hard, and I scratched his tummy where I knew he liked it.

And then Roxanne was beside me. She put a hand on my arm.

"I need you to tell me what to do," she said. "There's no one else I can ask, there's no one else I can trust."

"What is it?" I said.

"When they go tomorrow Niki wants me to go with him. I'm going to be a singer. Niki says I sing well enough to be famous. Do you think I do?"

"Of course you do," I said. It was an honest answer.

"I think I want to go, but I'm not sure. Grandpa says I should go because I'll be rich. He says that with the money I'll make, he could buy the farm next door. It will make all the difference, he says. And I do like singing. I do. You've always helped me, ever since I was little. Tell me what to do. Please."

Now I could speak out. Now was my chance. I could not believe the words I found myself uttering.

"You must do what you want, Roxanne," I said. "You're old enough to know what you want. I can't tell you what to do any more. No one can. It's your life."

She was looking at me – trying to drag the truth out of me. She wanted me to tell her to stay. She wanted me to stop her – I know she did. Then the moment passed.

"If I went," she said, "would you look after Bruno for me? And would you take him for walks sometimes? Would you?"

"If that's what you want, Roxanne," I said.

She leaned over and kissed me on the cheek.

"I knew you would," she said. "Then I shall go. I've talked to Bruno. I've told him. He understands." She turned to the bear. "You understand, don't you, Bruno? And anyway, Niki says I can come back whenever I want. And I'll come back often, honest I will. He says he'll take me to the sea. I've never seen the sea. We'll go up in planes. We'll fly. Can you imagine that?"

And then she was gone away from me, back towards the light of the café, back to Niki.

It was very late when Niki hushed everyone and told them the news I already knew. Roxanne stood beside him, looking down at her feet. Her grandfather had his arm around her and he was smiling like a cat that's got the cream. I think Niki expected applause when he had finished – he was rather used to applause – but the villagers were numbed to silence. The Mayor stood up and spoke for us because someone had to say something.

"Roxanne is a daughter to all of us," he said, "and no one likes to see a daughter leave. But we are proud of her, very proud; and we hope that wherever she goes, wherever she sings, she won't forget us or the place she belongs to."

It was Tiny who managed inadvertently to bring some smiles back. "Send us a postcard,

Roxy," he called out, and everyone laughed with relief. But there was no more dancing that night.

We were all there early the next morning and said our goodbyes to the film crew and to Roxanne. The Wardrobe Mistress kissed me fondly and said that she wished she'd had a teacher like me when she was at school. That was kind of her, I thought. Roxanne crouched down by Bruno's cage, a battered brown suitcase beside her. She clung to the bars.

"I'll be back," I heard her whisper. "I promise."

And then she got up and came over to me, wiping the tears from her eyes.

"Look after him for me," she said. Then she was gone.

They were all gone and we were left once more to ourselves, to the silence of our mountains.

Some time later that morning I went to give Bruno his breakfast. He was sitting back against the bars of the cage where Roxanne had left him, still gazing after her. I opened the door and poured his meal into his trough. He never moved. He never looked. It was only when I went to stroke him that I realised he was dead.

No one comes here much any more since Bruno died. From time to time I hear Roxanne singing with Niki on my radio, and I've seen her on the television too. She's almost more famous than he is, now. I feel proud and sad at the same time. She still sings like the angels. I wrote to her telling her about Bruno. She never replied. I'm sure she never even got the letter.

Some time ago, I received a parcel from the Wardrobe Mistress, and there was a note with it. She said she had told the Director of my passion for his purple fedora hat. Here it was, she said. It came with her love. It would be just right for me. I tried it on, but it did not fit.

Order Form

To order direct from the publishers, just make a list of the titles you want and fill in the form below:

Name ....

Address ....

....

....

Send to: Dept 6, HarperCollins Publishers Ltd, Westerhill Road, Bishopbriggs, Glasgow G64 2QT.

Please enclose a cheque or postal order to the value of the cover price, plus:

UK & BFPO: Add £1.00 for the first book, and 25p per copy for each additional book ordered.

Overseas and Eire: Add £2.95 service charge. Books will be sent by surface mail but quotes for airmail despatch will be given on request.

A 24-hour telephone ordering service is available to holders of Visa, MasterCard, Amex or Switch cards on 0141- 772 2281.

HarperCollins *Children's Books*